I Want to Learn to Fly!

A song composed and
sung by Maureen McGovern

Words by Judy Barron

Illustrations by Cyd Moore

SCHOLASTIC INC.

New York   Toronto   London   Auckland   Sydney

Music and lyrics copyright © 1995 by Maiden Voyage Music.
Illustrations copyright © 1995 by Cyd Moore.
All rights reserved. Published by Scholastic Inc.
Printed in the U.S.A.
ISBN 0-590-22329-1

4 5 6 7 8 9 10 11   40   07 06 05 04

For Megan,

the inspiration

– J.B.

More than anything else
In the world so wide,
More than anything
I want to learn to fly.

When I'm in school,
I'll hide my wings
From all the girls and boys.

And when I have to take a nap
Or put away my toys,

That's when I will spread my wings,
And up in the air I'll go...

Faster than the eye can see
Like an arrow from a bow!

More than anything else
In the world so wide,

More than anything
I want to learn to fly.

I'll fly to anywhere I want,
To places I've never seen,

Where grownups never, ever yell
And kids are never mean.

The food will be the things I like.
I'll never get sick or be scared again.

And everyone I meet will say,
"I want to be your friend!"

More than anything else
In the world so wide,

More than anything
I want to learn to fly.

I'll soar above the highest clouds
To Spain and Timbuktu,

And when I want a llama ride
I'll fly down to Peru.

For lunch I'll pick a mango
From a tree beside the Nile,

And take off just before I'm caught
By a toothy crocodile.

More than anything else
In the world so wide,
More than anything
I want to learn to fly.

I'll find a desert made of sand
And build a castle there,

And then a deep dark jungle filled
With parrots darting everywhere.

A chimpanzee with bright green eyes

Will play with me and be my friend.

And then before the nighttime comes

More than anything else
In the world so wide,
More than anything
I want to learn to fly.

I Want to Learn to Fly!

Music by Maureen McGovern

Lyrics Judy Barro[n]

3. I'll soar above the highest clouds
   To Spain and Timbuktu,
   And when I want a llama ride
   I'll fly down to Peru.
   For lunch I'll pick a mango
   From a tree beside the Nile,
   And take off just before I'm caught
   By a toothy crocodile.

4. I'll find a desert made of sand
   And build a castle there,
   And then a jungle filled
   With parrots darting everywhere.
   A chimpanzee with bright green eyes
   Will play and be my friend.
   And then before the nighttime comes
   We'll fly back home again.

Music and lyrics copyright © 1995 by Maiden Voyage Music.

We'll fly back home again.